BRANCH'S BUNKER BIRTHDAY

BY David Lewman
Illustrated by Alan Batson

 A GOLDEN BOOK • NEW YORK

DreamWorks Trolls © 2018 DreamWorks Animation LLC. All Rights Reserved. Published in the United States by Golden Books, an imprint of Random House Children's Books, a division of Penguin Random House LLC, 1745 Broadway, New York, NY 10019, and in Canada by Penguin Random House Canada Limited, Toronto. Golden Books, A Golden Book, A Little Golden Book, the G colophon, and the distinctive gold spine are registered trademarks of Penguin Random House LLC.

rhcbooks.com

ISBN 978-1-5247-7260-4 (trade) — ISBN 978-1-5247-7261-1 (ebook)

Printed in the United States of America
10 9 8 7 6 5 4 3 2 1

Poppy was so excited! Tomorrow was her friend **BRANCH'S BIRTHDAY!**

Poppy ran to Branch's bunker and knocked.

KNOCK!

KNOCK!

KNOCK!

Inside the bunker, Poppy showed Branch
the invitation she'd made.

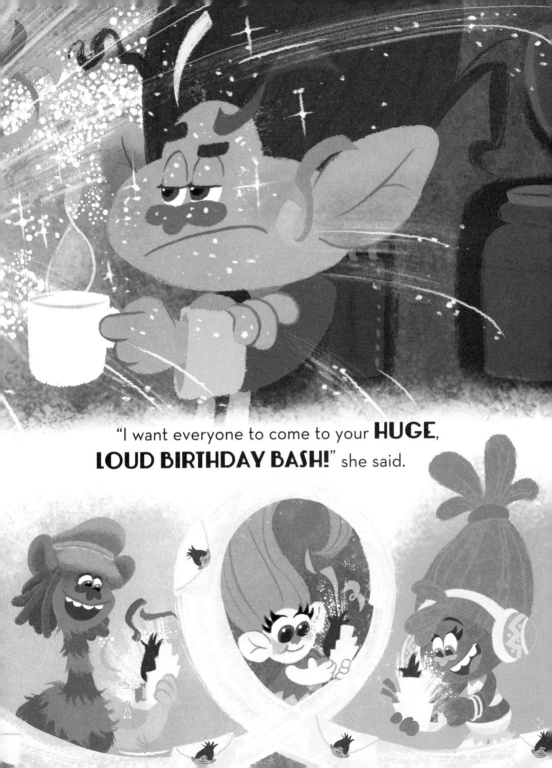

"I want everyone to come to your **HUGE, LOUD BIRTHDAY BASH!**" she said.

"No thank you," Branch said.

"I don't like **BIG**
parties!

I don't like **LOUD**
parties!

I don't like
BIRTHDAY
parties!

I just want a quiet, peaceful day
to myself—alone."

Poppy couldn't believe it. Alone? On his birthday? She thought Branch had changed when they'd made friends with the Bergens, but now it seemed as though the "new" Branch was an awful lot like the "old" Branch!

The next morning, Branch woke up early and made himself breakfast. It was quiet in his bunker.

A little TOO quiet.

So he decided to go for a nice, peaceful birthday walk. He headed toward the center of Troll Village, quietly singing, *"Happy birthday to me. . . ."*

At the cupcakery, Biggie was making lots of cupcakes.

"What are all these cupcakes for?" Branch asked.

"Um . . . the **TROLLS CUPCAKE FESTIVAL!**" Biggie said.

"Oh," Branch said. "I've never heard of that festival!"

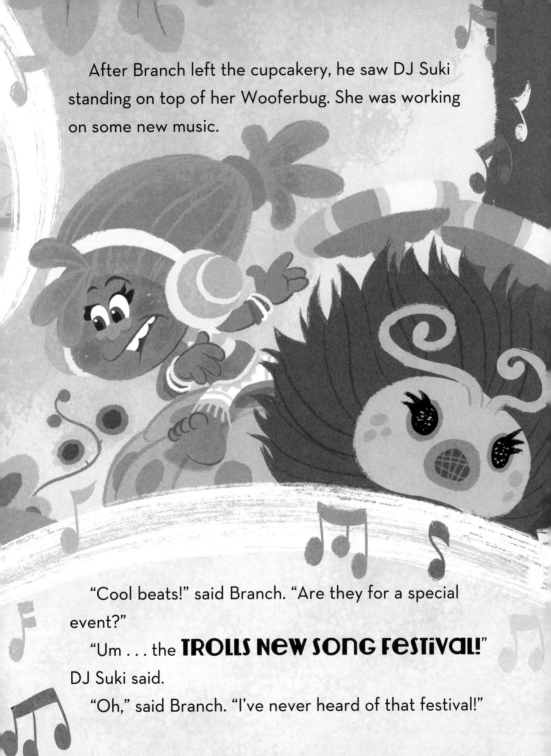

After Branch left the cupcakery, he saw DJ Suki standing on top of her Wooferbug. She was working on some new music.

"Cool beats!" said Branch. "Are they for a special event?"

"Um . . . the **TROLLS NEW SONG FESTIVAL!**" DJ Suki said.

"Oh," said Branch. "I've never heard of that festival!"

Next, Branch went to visit Satin and Chenille.
They were making new outfits.

"Are those for a festival?" Branch asked.

"No," said Satin. "They're for . . ."

"NEW OUTFIT DAY!" Chenille said quickly.

"Oh," Branch said. "Never heard of it."

In her salon, Maddy was giving Smidge and Sierra new hairdos.

"Are you getting your hair done for a special occasion?" Branch asked.

"NOPE!"

"NOPE!"

"NOPE!"

In her studio, Harper was working on a new painting.

"It's for the . . . um . . . **TROLLS ART FAIR!**" she explained.

"May I see it?" Branch asked.

"It's not ready yet," Harper insisted.

As Branch continued on his walk, he saw Cooper carrying a big box of presents.

"Who are all those presents for?" Branch asked.

"Who knows?" Cooper said. "I just deliver 'em!"

Branch shrugged and decided to head home.

When he walked into his bunker,
all his friends were there.

"I know you said you wanted to spend your birthday alone," said Poppy, "but I just **KNEW** you'd love a party with your friends!"

"You know what, Poppy?" Branch said. "You were . . ."